For my two little birds,
who have left the nest.
— *M.N.D.*

Published in 2014 by Eerdmans Books for Young Readers,
an imprint of Wm. B. Eerdmans Publishing Co.
2140 Oak Industrial Dr. NE
Grand Rapids, Michigan 49505
P.O. Box 163, Cambridge CB3 9PU U.K.
www.eerdmans.com/youngreaders
Manufactured at Tien Wah Press
in Malaysia in July 2013, first printing
20 19 18 17 16 15 14   9 8 7 6 5 4 3 2 1

Library of Congress Cataloging-in-Publication Data

DePalma, Mary Newell, author, illustrator.
Two little birds / by Mary Newell DePalma; illustrated by
Mary Newell DePalma.
pages cm
Summary: Two little birds make their first grand migration south, and
later return home to start new families.
ISBN 978-0-8028-5421-6
1. Birds — Migration — Juvenile fiction. [1. Birds — Migration — Fiction.]
I. Title.
PZ10.3.D418Tw 2014
[E] — dc23
2013024835

The illustrations were rendered in mixed media collage.
The text type was set in Filmotype MacBeth.

Special thanks to Gayle Levée for
my adaptation of her drawing
"Night Migrations," the lower
left vignette on page 27.

Two Little Birds

Written and illustrated by

Mary Newell DePalma

Eerdmans Books for Young Readers

Grand Rapids, Michigan • Cambridge, U.K.

After much effort . . . .

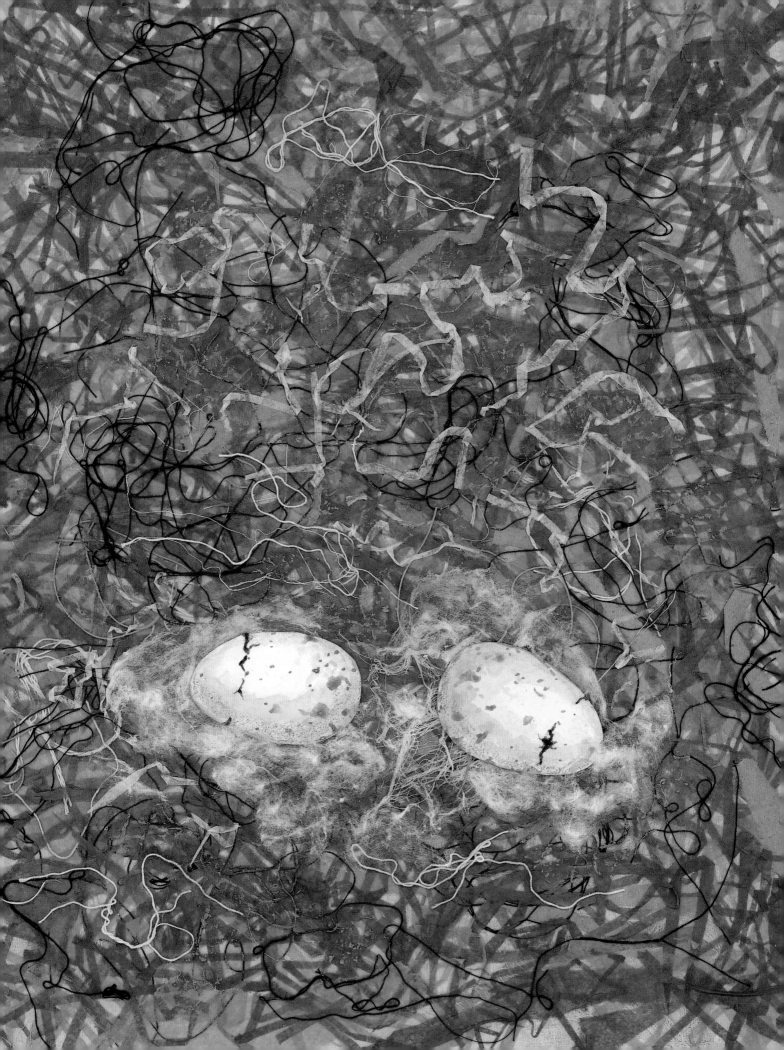

.... two little birds
emerged from their eggs.

"It's very bright!"

"There's lots of room!"

The little birds did
what little birds do.

They fed,

they frolicked,

they grew.

One night they saw
an amazing sight.

"Ahhh!"

"Let's go too!"

They flew,

and flew,

and flew.

They flew beyond
all they knew.

rumble

flash

boom!

The little birds tumbled,
the little birds tossed.

The little birds did
what little birds do.
They skipped,
they scouted,
they flew.

They flew,

and flew,

and flew.

"Now what do we do?"

flap! flap! flap!

Hours passed.

flap! flap! flap!

Their wings ached.

flap! flap! flap!

It hurt to breathe.

flap! flap! flap!
flap! flap! flap!

"You can do it!"

"I don't know…"

Whew!

The flutter and chatter
of many birds
woke them up.

The little birds did
what little birds do.
They fed,
they frolicked,
they discovered
what's new.

"Mmmm, this is good!"

"This is too!"

After a while,
the young birds
thought of home.
They remembered a cozy nest,
delicious grasshoppers,
and the songs
their father taught them.

"It's so far . . ."

"But we are strong!"

After much effort,
the strong young birds
arrived home.

Then these birds did
what all birds do.
They sang,
they snuggled . . .

. . . they started something new.

From the Author

Every year, millions of birds migrate, making their way across continents and oceans. My story is loosely based on the annual migration of orchard orioles from the northeastern United States to Central America and back. Orioles migrate at night with thousands of other songbirds. When they reach the southern edge of the United States, these tiny creatures somehow summon the strength to fly continuously for eighteen hours across the Gulf of Mexico to the Yucatán Peninsula. A few months later, they repeat this dangerous and exciting adventure when they return to their nesting grounds in the north.

We share our planet with these indomitable little individuals, and yet there is still much we do not know about bird migration. Be curious! We journey together.

Mary Newell DePalma